I AM READING

Ooh La La, Lottie!

KAREN WALLACE

ILLUSTRATED BY
GARRY PARSONS

KINGFISHER
BOSTON

Dedicated to Gracie—K. W.
Pour Monsieur Cazier—G. P.

KINGFISHER
a Houghton Mifflin Company imprint
222 Berkeley Street
Boston, Massachusetts 02116
www.houghtonmifflinbooks.com

First published in 2004
ITR/0604/AJT/GRS(GRS)/115SMA

2 4 6 8 10 9 7 5 3 1

LIBRARY OF CONGRESS CATALOGING-IN-PUBLICATION DATA
has been applied for.

ISBN 0-7534-5716-4

Printed in India

Contents

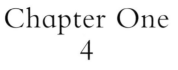

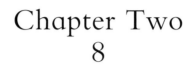
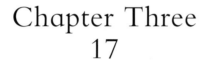

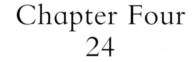
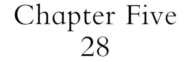

Chapter One

Once there was a girl named Lottie
La Belle.

She lived with her mother and father
and a big white poodle named Patrick.

Lottie had thick black hair and
eyes as brown as chestnuts.

She always had her hair in pigtails.
She didn't care what clothes she wore.
Lottie was only interested
in one thing. She loved
playing with Patrick.

Every day Lottie made Patrick a new
clip-on bow tie for his collar.

Every day Patrick walked with Lottie
to school.

And when she did her homework,
he lay under her desk and kept her
feet warm.
When she went swimming, he watched
from the bleachers.

Chapter Two

One evening Lottie sat down to dinner
in a bad mood. Her pants were ripped,
and the buttons were missing from her
shirt. Her hair looked like she had cut
it with a pair of garden shears.

"Ooh la la, Lottie!" cried Mrs. La Belle. "You look like something the cat dragged in."

Lottie glared at her mother. She was so annoyed that she wanted to do something really naughty.

9

On the table was broccoli in a cream sauce with buttered peas, carrots, and fresh green beans.

It was Lottie's favorite dinner, but now she didn't care.

Lottie pushed her plate away.

"Patrick hates vegetables. So do I."

Mr. La Belle twitched his mustache.

"Will you eat dog food then?" he
asked sternly.

On the other side of the room was a plate
of cheese and crackers.

A brilliant idea popped into Lottie's mind.

"Of course I won't eat dog food," said
Lottie. "I will eat bread and cheese.
Patrick likes cheese," she added quickly.
Mrs. La Belle rolled her eyes.

"Ooh la la, Lottie!" she cried.
"What will you think of next?"
From that moment on Lottie La Belle
only ate bread and cheese.

She ate bread and
cheese for breakfast.

She ate bread and
cheese for lunch.

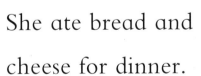

She ate bread and
cheese for dinner.

It was the same the next week and the week after that.

"Don't you get tired of eating bread and cheese?" asked her friend Jeanette.

"No," said Lottie. "I like it."

She smiled, and Jeanette noticed
something strange.

Lottie's front teeth had grown long
and sharp.

Her ears were strangely furry.

That night Lottie didn't sleep in her bed.
She curled up on top of a pile of leaves
she had hidden in her closet.

Chapter Three

The next day Lottie had a piano lesson.

But when Lottie sat down on the

bench, the teacher's eyes popped out

of his head.

A tail was hanging out from the hem

of Lottie's skirt!

In the afternoon Lottie painted a picture of herself. When the teacher saw it, she jumped onto a chair and screamed. It was a picture of a mouse!

Lottie's parents were called to the school immediately.

"I'm sorry to inform you that your daughter has turned into a mouse," said the principal.

"Ooh la la, Lottie!" cried Mrs. La Belle. "What will we do?"

"Take her to the vet," said the principal.

"No child of mine will go to a vet," shouted Mr. La Belle. "She might catch fleas in the waiting room! I will take her to a doctor immediately."

The doctor counted Lottie's whiskers.

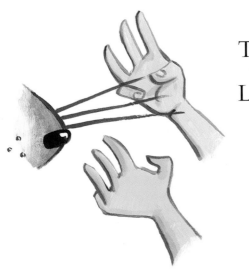

She shone a flashlight in Lottie's furry ears.

She measured the length of Lottie's tail.

"She is definitely a mouse," the doctor
said.

"What will we do?" cried
Mrs. La Belle.

"She must not eat any more cheese,"
said the doctor firmly.

"She must eat only vegetables."

"But I like being a mouse," said
Lottie La Belle.

And she scampered out of the room
before anyone could catch her.

Chapter Four

It didn't matter what kind of
vegetables Mrs. La Belle cooked.
It didn't matter whether they were
raw, fried, steamed, or baked.
Lottie would not eat them.
After awhile Mrs. La Belle gave up.

She swept the leaves out from her daughter's closet instead of making her bed. She even cut holes in Lottie's pants so that her tail would be more comfortable.

Mr. La Belle gave up too. He didn't
read Lottie fairy tales anymore.
She didn't like them because the princes
and princesses weren't mice.

So Mr. La Belle read her mouse
adventures and changed the endings
so that the mice always won.

As for Patrick, he was very sad because Lottie didn't play with him anymore. She was too busy making nests under the sofa or looking for crumbs on the floor.

Poor Patrick! Most days he lay outside the back door.

Chapter Five

One day Lottie's friend Jeanette came to visit.

"Why don't you come to school anymore?" she asked.

Lottie crawled out from behind the sofa.

"Mice don't go to school," she said as she nibbled on a piece of cheese. "Mice don't like schoolwork."

Jeanette stared at her feet.

"Do mice like swimming?" she asked at last.

Lottie cocked her head to one side and pulled thoughtfully on a whisker.

"I'm not sure."

Mrs. La Belle looked up from where she was cutting out mouse-shaped cookies.

"Ooh la la, Lottie!" she cried. "Of course mice like swimming!"

Patrick lifted
Lottie's swimming
bag from its hook
in the hall and
stood in the kitchen
wagging his tail.

"Okay," said Lottie. "I will go."

So Lottie and Jeanette went to the pool,
and Patrick sat in the
bleachers. A moment
later Jeanette
jumped into
the pool.

Lottie stood by the side. She looked at the
water, and suddenly she felt very afraid.
Her mother wasn't right at all!

"Lottie!" cried Jeanette.

"What's wrong?"

"Mice do NOT like swimming!" shouted Lottie.

And without another word, she disappeared.

Chapter Six

One day Lottie was sitting in the backyard chewing on an apple seed.

An apple seed was very big for Lottie because as time passed she had become smaller and smaller.

Now she was more like a mouse than ever.

Lottie swallowed the apple seed and
bit into another.

She didn't take much notice when the
cat from next door sat down beside her.
Then he moved closer, and she smelled
his hot, hungry, catty breath.

Suddenly, she knew she was in danger!

"Help! Help!" shouted Lottie. "The cat wants to eat me!"

But Mrs. La Belle didn't hear because Lottie's shout was only as loud as a mouse's squeak.

Lottie jumped up and ran across the grass.

The cat ran after her.

"Help! Help!" she cried again.

This time Patrick pricked up his ears.

Quick as a flash he jumped

onto the grass.

Then he chased the cat away just as it
was about to gobble up Lottie!

Lottie lay on the ground and howled.

Patrick howled too.

He hated to see

Lottie unhappy.

Mrs. La Belle ran into the yard.

"I don't want to be a mouse anymore," sobbed Lottie. "I want to be a little girl again."

Mrs. La Belle kissed Lottie's furry pink ears.

"Then you must do what the doctor told you," she said.

Chapter Seven

The doctor was right.

After a week of eating her vegetables

Lottie was almost a little girl again.

One day, when she was completely
better, Lottie came down for dinner.
On the table was broccoli in a cream
sauce with buttered peas, carrots,
and fresh green beans.

"Yum! Vegetables!" cried Lottie.

"I love vegetables!"

And she helped herself to lots of
everything.

Mr. La Belle twitched his mustache.

"What about Patrick?" he asked,
slowly. "You said he hated vegetables."

"Patrick has changed his mind!" said Lottie La Belle with a grin. She put down her knife and fork and whistled.

Patrick trotted into the room with a huge

carrot in his mouth.

Lottie had cut it into the shape of a bone!

Mr. La Belle burst out laughing.

"Ooh la la, Lottie!" cried Mrs. La Belle.

"What will you think of next?"

About the author and illustrator

Karen Wallace is an award-winning writer and has published more than 90 books for children.

"*Ooh La La, Lottie!* was based on a little girl I met in France when my son was on an exchange visit," says Karen. "I love writing funny books because I get to laugh at my own jokes."

Garry Parsons is an illustrator of children's books, magazines, and advertisements. He likes to draw and paint all day long. Garry says, "Like Lottie, I love eating lots of bread and cheese too. I wonder what animal she would have turned into if she had eaten a lot of something else, like bananas or sardines!"

Strategies for Independent Readers

Predict
Think about the cover, illustrations, and the title
of the book. What do you think this book will be about?
While you are reading think about what may
happen next and why.

Monitor
As you read ask yourself if what you're
reading makes sense. If it doesn't, reread, look
at the illustrations, or read ahead.

Question
Ask yourself questions about important ideas
in the story such as what the characters might
do or what you might learn.

Phonics
If there is a word that you do not know, look carefully
at the letters, sounds, and word parts that you do know.
Blend the sounds to read the word. Ask yourself if this is
a word you know. Does it make sense in the sentence?

Summarize
Think about the characters, the setting where the
story takes place, and the problem the characters faced
in the story. Tell the important ideas in the beginning,
middle, and end of the story.

Evaluate
Ask yourself questions like: Did you like the story?
Why or why not? How did the author make the story
come alive? How did the author make the story fun to
read? How well did you understand the story? Maybe
you can understand it better if you read it again!